Stories Are Magic

Stories Are Magic

Little, Brown and Company

New York Boston

Headlines set in Generation B by Harold's Fonts.

My Little Pony: We Like Spike! originally published in September 2015 by Little, Brown and Company
My Little Pony: Pinkie Pie Keeps a Secret originally published in April 2016 by Little, Brown and Company
My Little Pony: Meet Starlight Glimmer originally published in January 2017 by Little, Brown and Company
My Little Pony: We Are Family originally published in April 2017 by Little, Brown and Company

Cover design by Cassie Gonzales

Little, Brown and Company
Hachette Book Group
1290 Avenue of the Americas, New York, NY 10104
Visit us at LBYR.com
mylittlepony.com

First Bindup Edition: November 2017

ISBNs: 978-0-316-48017-8 (hardcover)

PRINTED IN CHINA

RRD-S

10 9 8 7 6 5 4 3 2 1

Passport to Reading titles are leveled by independent reviewers applying the standards developed by Irene Fountas and Gay Su Pinnell in *Matching Books to Readers: Using Leveled Books in Guided Reading*, Heinemann, 1999.

Licensed By:

Table of Contents

We Like Spike!   1

Pinkie Pie Keeps A Secret   31

Meet Starlight Glimmer   61

We Are Family   91

MY LITTLE PONY

WE LIKE SPIKE!

Written by **Jennifer Fox**

LITTLE, BROWN AND COMPANY
New York Boston

Attention, My Little Pony fans!
Look for these words when you read this book.
Can you spot them all?

dragon

breath

heroes

gem

What is purple and green
and came from a tiny egg?

It is our friend Spike!

He is a dragon.

Spike is not big or scary
like other dragons.

He is a cute little guy.

He is a great friend
and a super assistant.

Spike uses his magic fire breath
to send scrolls.

He is always ready to help.

Spike works really hard.

He also knows how to have fun!

17

Spike likes to read comic books.

His favorite heroes
are the Power Ponies.

He likes to laugh and
can be very silly!

Our little Spike is
a total sweetheart.

He also has a big sweet tooth!

Spike bakes yummy gem cakes.

Most of the gems do not
end up in the cake!
They end up in his belly!

Spike is not a pony,
but he is family.

We like Spike!

![My Little Pony logo]

PINKIE PIE KEEPS A SECRET

Adapted by **Magnolia Belle**

Based on the episode
"The One Where Pinkie Pie Knows"

Written by **Gillian M. Berrow**

LITTLE, BROWN AND COMPANY
New York   Boston

Attention, My Little Pony fans!
Look for these words when you read this book.
Can you spot them all?

cupcakes

disguise

snacks

certificate

Pinkie Pie is making cupcakes at
Sugarcube Corner when Mrs. Cake
gets a special letter.

The letter says Princess Cadance
and Shining Armor want a cake
for their brand-new baby!

Mrs. Cake tells Pinkie Pie
that the new baby is a secret.
Pinkie Pie gulps.
"I have to keep a secret!"

Later, Pinkie Pie joins her friends
in Twilight Sparkle's castle.
The princess has news!

Twilight says that she is throwing a party
for her big brother, Shining Armor, and
Princess Cadance.

"And?" Pinkie Pie asks.

Twilight says that is all the news.

Pinkie Pie still has
to keep the secret.

The friends decorate the castle
as a surprise for Shining Armor.
Talking about surprises makes
Pinkie Pie scared.
She is afraid she will tell the secret!

Twilight Sparkle finds a toy
that Shining Armor used to
play with as a baby.
Hearing the word "baby"
makes Pinkie Pie scared, too.

She asks the other ponies
if it is okay to tell a secret.

Rarity says no.

Pinkie Pie thinks she needs to
be alone to keep the secret.

Back at Sugarcube Corner,

Mr. Cake asks her to deliver orders.

Pinkie Pie is scared.

How will she keep the secret?

First, Pinkie Pie wears a disguise.

The Cutie Mark Crusaders can

tell it is their friend.

They ask if there is any news.

"Nope!" she says.

Next, Pinkie Pie sees Fluttershy. She asks Pinkie Pie to bring snacks like baby carrots to the party.

"Baby carrots?"

Pinkie Pie runs away.

Pinkie Pie decides the only way to keep a secret is to stay away from everypony.

Every time she sees another pony,

she zips by before they can say hello.

After she is done, Pinkie Pie is tired.
She still has to go to the party.

Pinkie Pie brings snacks
to the castle.
All the ponies are busy
getting ready.

Soon, Princess Cadance
and Shining Armor arrive
for the party!

Shining Armor has a game

for the ponies.

Twilight and her friends have

to find clues.

All the clues will reveal a surprise!

Shining Armor says that the first clue
is "where young ones spend their week."
The ponies think.

They find a clue in the schoolhouse!
It says to look at Applejack's birth
certificate.
Pinkie Pie dashes to the town hall.

The next clue says they need to "find a
place to buy comfy beds for little heads."
They need to find a baby crib!

The next clue tells them to "take a break where they can get a slice of cake."

The ponies go to Sugarcube Corner
and find Shining Armor and
Princess Cadance!
Princess Cadance tells Twilight to think
about what the clues have in common.

Twilight Sparkle looks at the clues: the schoolhouse, Applejack's birth certificate, a baby crib.

Twilight gasps!

Princess Cadance and Shining Armor
announce, "We are having a baby!"

Twilight Sparkle asks,

"I am going to be an aunt?

That is the best surprise ever!"

Pinkie Pie is so happy.

"I did it!

I kept the secret!" she cries.

Everypony celebrates the good news
with cake!
Princess Cadance thanks Pinkie Pie
for keeping the secret.
Pinkie Pie laughs.
"Aw, it was a piece of cake."

Meet Starlight Glimmer

Written by **Magnolia Belle**

LITTLE, BROWN AND COMPANY

New York Boston

Attention, My Little Pony fans!
Look for these words when you read this book.
Can you spot them all?

cutie mark

mess

picnic

relax

Starlight Glimmer is a new
Unicorn in Ponyville.
She learns about magic from
Princess Twilight Sparkle.

Starlight Glimmer loves to learn.
She learns a lot about being
a good friend.

Starlight did not always
want to be a good friend.
She was not nice.

One time, she used magic

to give all ponies

the same cutie mark!

Another time, she tried to stop

Rainbow Dash's Sonic Rainboom.

Twilight saved the day!
She told Starlight about
the Magic of Friendship
and invited her to Ponyville.

Twilight helped Starlight
make new friends with Pinkie Pie,
Rainbow Dash, Fluttershy,
Applejack, and Rarity.

Starlight remembers her old friend Sunburst.
He moved to Canterlot to study magic.

Starlight gets to see Sunburst today!

She is excited, but she is also nervous.

Starlight and Sunburst are both shy.

They do not talk at first.

Starlight uses her magic
to help Sunburst.
They are not shy anymore!

Starlight and Sunburst are
good friends!

Twilight is proud of Starlight
for being a good friend to Sunburst.
Starlight wants to make more friends!

Starlight explores Ponyville
to find a new friend.

First, she bakes cakes
with Pinkie Pie and Mrs. Cake.
Her magic makes a mess.
Mrs. Cake is not happy.

Next, Starlight picks apples
with Applejack and Big Mac.
Her magic scares Big Mac.

Then Starlight visits Rarity.

They play dress-up.

Rarity says dressing up

is a good way to make friends.

Finally, Starlight has a picnic
with Fluttershy.

Starlight has a good day
but is sad she does not
meet new friends.

She visits Ponyville Spa to relax.

She needs to stop worrying.

At the spa,

Starlight meets Trixie.

She is nice!

Trixie once did mean things,
but she wants to be
a good friend now,
just like Starlight.

Starlight is so excited.
She tells Twilight
about her new friend.

Some ponies worry
about Starlight's new friend.
They do not know
Trixie is not mean anymore.

Starlight is a good friend to Trixie.

She says she is a good pony.

The new friends put on a great
magic show together.

Starlight Glimmer is happy
to have a new friend.
They really share the
Magic of Friendship!

We Are Family

Written by **Magnolia Belle**

LITTLE, BROWN AND COMPANY
New York Boston

Attention, My Little Pony fans!
Look for these words when you read this book.
Can you spot them all?

Castle of Friendship

magic

bakery

sports teams

In Ponyville, family is as
important as friendship!

Twilight Sparkle is a
part of many families.

Twilight lives in the Castle of Friendship
with Spike.

He is her best friend!

She also lives with her pet,
Owlowiscious.

Twilight loves Spike and Owlowiscious.
They are a family!

Twilight loves her parents, too.
She is great at magic because
her parents are Unicorns, too!

Twilight has a brother.
Shining Armor is married
to Princess Cadance.

They have a baby named Flurry Heart.
Twilight is Flurry Heart's aunt!

Flurry Heart is not the only baby
in Equestria.

Mr. and Mrs. Cake's twins are named
Pound Cake and Pumpkin Cake.

Fluttershy also has a brother.
His name is Zephyr Breeze.

Twilight and Fluttershy do not have
sisters, but Pinkie Pie has three!
They work with their parents.

Rarity also has a little sister.

She is very helpful.

Her name is Sweetie Belle.

Applejack has a brother and sister.

Big McIntosh and Apple Bloom

live with Granny Smith.

She takes good care of them.

Rainbow Dash does not have
a sister or brother.
She is an only child.
She looks out for Scootaloo
like a big sister.

Sometimes brothers and sisters fight
and hurt one another's feelings.
And sometimes they are the
best of friends.

Princess Celestia and Princess Luna
were mad at each other.
Now they are friends again.

Sometimes families live together
or get together for parties...

...like the Apple family.

And sometimes the ponies and friends who live together become a family, like Twilight and Spike.

Fluttershy has lots of pets.

She treats them like family.

They love Fluttershy very much.

Opalescence is Rarity's cat.

She is part of her family.

Pinkie lives with the Cake family.

She works with them in their bakery.

They help one another like family.

Sports teams are another
kind of family.
The Wonderbolts train
together every day.

Best friends are also like a family.
The Cutie Mark Crusaders are
like sisters.

Twilight, Applejack, Fluttershy, Rarity, Pinkie, Rainbow Dash, and Spike are close friends and make up a special family.

No matter where a pony lives,
they are with their family
when they feel love.

The End